For Elsie and Emile —M. R.

For Rebecca —A. R.

Text copyright © 2007 by Michael Rosen
Illustrations copyright © 2007 by Adrian Reynolds

Typeset in Temble ITC
Art created with watercolor

First published in Great Britain in 2007 by Bloomsbury Publishing Plc.
Published in the United States in 2007 by Bloomsbury U.S.A. Children's Books
175 Fifth Avenue, New York, NY 10010
Distributed to the trade by Holtzbrinck Publishers

Library of Congress Cataloging-in-Publication Data
Rosen, Michael.
Bear's day out / by Michael Rosen ; illustrations by Adrian Reynolds. — 1st U.S. ed.
p.     cm.
Summary: When Bear decides to visit the city, he becomes overwhelmed with all
the noise, but luckily some helpful children guide him on his way home again.
ISBN-13: 978-1-59990-007-0 • ISBN-10: 1-59990-007-6
[1. Bears—Fiction. 2. Sound—Fiction. 3. Friendship—Fiction.]
I. Reynolds, Adrian, ill. II. Title.
PZ7.R71867Be 2007      [E]—dc22      2007001441

First U.S. Edition 2007
Printed in China
1 3 5 7 9 10 8 6 4 2

# Bear's Day Out

Michael Rosen • illustrated by Adrian Reynolds

BLOOMSBURY
CHILDREN'S
BOOKS

I'm a bear in a cave.
In a cave?
In a cave.

I'm a bear all alone.
All alone?
All alone.

And I sing to myself all day.
Doo bee doo
Doo bee doo
Doo bee doodily doo.

I walk by the sea.
By the sea?
By the sea!

And I play in the waves all day.
Splishy splash
Splishy splash
Splishy splashy splish.

But then I heard a noise.
Heard a noise?
Heard a noise!

It came from far away.
Far away?
Far away!

The sound of the city filled my ears.
Vroomy vroom
Vroomy vroom
Vroomy vroomy vroom.

I got a ticket to the city.
To the city?
To the city!

And I traveled to the city far away.
Chuffy chuff
Chuffy chuff
Chuffy chuffity chuff.

I saw buildings in the sky.
In the sky?
In the sky!

I saw people rushing by.
Rushing by?
Rushing by!

And the cars flew by all day.
Whooshy whoosh
Whooshy whoosh
Whooshy whooshy whoosh.

I went to the market.
To the market?
To the market!

Bananas, fish, and shoes.
Fish and shoes?
Fish and shoes!

With people shouting out,
"You gotta buy *this*!"
"You gotta buy *that*!"
"You gotta buy *this* and *that*!"

I ran to the park.
To the park?
To the park!

I sat on a swing.
On a swing?
On a swing!

But people laughed at me.
Hee hee hee
Ha ha ha
Hee hee ha ha ha.

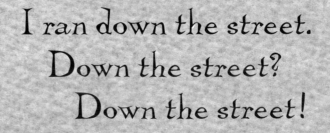

I ran down the street.
Down the street?
Down the street!

I sat on a bench.
On a bench?
On a bench!

I heard some people coming near.
They said, "It's a bear!"
"It's a bear?"
"It's a bear!"

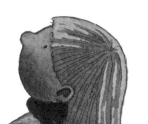

"It looks like it's lost."
"Like it's lost?"
"Like it's lost!"

"Let's take it home."
"Follow us!"
"Follow us!"
"Follow us, us, us!"

Through the park.
Hee hee hee
Ha ha ha
Hee hee ha ha ha.

Through the market.
"Buy this!"
"Buy that!"
"You must buy this and that!"

Past the cars.
Whooshy whoosh
Whooshy whoosh
Whooshy whooshy whoosh.

On the train.
Chuffy chuff.
Chuffy chuff.
Chuffy chuffity chuff.

The city in my ears.
Vroomy vroom
Vroomy vroom
Vroomy vroomy vroom.

To play in the waves.
Splishy splash
Splishy splash
Splishy splashy splish.

To sing together all day.

Doo bee doo, doo bee

doo, doo bee doodily doo.